EGG-DROP
D · A · Y

BY HARRIET ZIEFERT
ILLUSTRATED BY
RICHARD BROWN

MR ROSE

LITTLE, BROWN AND COMPANY   BOSTON   TORONTO

Sally

Mr. Rose's Class

Jennifer

Richard

Adam

Emily

First Edition

Library of Congress Cataloging-in-Publication Data
Ziefert, Harriet
  Egg-drop day.
  (Mr. Rose's class)
  Summary: The students in Mr. Rose's science class
have a contest to see whose wrapped egg can survive the
drop from a window.
  [1. Schools—Fiction.   2. Contests—Fiction]
I. Brown, Richard Eric, 1946– ill. II. Title.
III. Series: Ziefert, Harriet.   Mr. Rose's class.
PZ7.Z487Eg   1988   [E]   87-3125
ISBN 0-316-98757-3

Published simultaneously in Canada
by Little, Brown & Company (Canada) Limited

Printed in Singapore for Harriet Ziefert, Inc.

For my first teachers—
Samuel Margolin, Sylvia Margolin,
Isaac Godlin, Helen Hudak

CHAPTER ONE
RAW EGGS

"Good morning, class! It's Thursday,"
said Mr. Rose.
"Good morning, Mr. Rose."
"Are you all ready for a special
announcement?"
"We're all ready, Mr. Rose!"

"Today we're going to have an egg-drop
        contest," Mr. Rose said.
"What's that?" Sarah asked.
"Give me a chance to explain,"
        answered Mr. Rose.
    He took an egg carton from a paper bag
    and held it up for everyone to see.
    Mr. Rose said, "I'm going to give each
        of you an egg."
"Are the eggs cooked?" Matt asked.
"No, they're raw," Mr. Rose answered.
        "I challenge each of you to wrap
        your egg well enough so that when I drop it
        out the window, it will hit the ground
        without breaking."
"He must be kidding!" whispered Kelly.
"It's impossible!" added Matt.
"Maybe not," said Sarah. "Mr. Rose usually
        knows what he's doing."

9

"How many tries do we get?" Emily asked.

"Only one!" Mr. Rose answered.

Everyone moaned.

But Emily knew one try was fair—otherwise
Mr. Rose wouldn't have enough eggs.

"Are there prizes?" Sarah asked.

"Unbroken eggs!" said Mr. Rose.
"We can cook them for a snack."

"Eggs for a snack! That sounds disgusting!"
yelled Richard.

"It's not disgusting," said Sarah.
"I like eggs."

"Yeah," said Sally. "It's something different
for a change. Maybe we can have a party.
Can we, Mr. Rose?" Sally begged.

"We'll see," Mr. Rose answered. "If everything
goes well and you all work hard today,
then the answer is yes."

Everyone clapped.

"Remember," said Mr. Rose, "we'll have a party
only if you do some good thinking today."

Jamie said to Adam, "What do you think
the contest is going to prove?"
"What do you mean?" asked Adam.
"I bet Mr. Rose is going to teach us
something about gravity," Jamie said.
Adam shrugged. "Could be. You never know
with Mr. Rose."

Matt turned to Richard.
"This contest shouldn't be too hard," he said.
Richard reminded Matt that their classroom
was on the second floor.
"I'll bet we're twenty—maybe even fifty—
feet above the ground," Richard said.

Sarah looked at Sally.

They were both thinking how nice
it would be to win.

"I hope my egg doesn't break," Sarah said.

"Me, too," said Sally.

"I'd be so embarrassed if it did,"
Sarah added.

"You shouldn't be," said Sally. "Mr. Rose
says what you learn is what matters.
Not if you win or lose."

"I guess so," said Sarah. "But I still hope
I don't break an egg today!"

Mr. Rose called everyone
to the science table.
He showed them what they might use
to solve the problem.
There was string, rubber bands, newspaper,
and all kinds of boxes.
There was wool, cotton, and foam rubber.
There was tape, salt, and clay.
There were even tennis balls!
Matt asked, "Can we use anything we want?"
"Anything," Mr. Rose answered. "Use as much
or as little as you need. You each have
thirty minutes to wrap your egg. Or,
you can put it inside a package or anything
else you can think of."

Everyone started to grab at the stuff.
Matt held onto a whole block of clay.
Emily took all the cotton.
Justin and Sarah were fighting over
a ball of twine.
"I got it first!" yelled Sarah, who would
    not let go of one end of the string.
Mr. Rose shouted, "FREEZE!"
He made everyone sit down.
He said, "I want you to think quietly
    about what you are going to do.
    When you have a plan, let me know.
    Then you can take what you need."

Maybe this wasn't going to be
as easy as it sounded.
Jennifer was the first to talk to Mr. Rose.
Matt whispered to Kelly, "She always
has to be first!"
Richard, who looked worried, waited
behind Jennifer.
He asked Mr. Rose a question.
Then he left the classroom.
Everyone wondered where he went.
"I thought we could only use what you put
on the table," Matt said to Mr. Rose.
"If you have another idea," answered Mr. Rose,
"talk to me. I'll tell you if you can
get something from somewhere else."

One by one, each person went to the table
and collected stuff.
"Be careful of the eggs!" Mr. Rose said.
    "Only one egg to a customer!"
Adam said, "I wonder who's going to be
    the first to break an egg?"
Matt was sure it would be Justin.
He was always doing something wrong.
But maybe this would be a day of surprises.
Probably yes.
Egg-Drop Day—a day of surprises.

CHAPTER TWO
GETTING READY

Mr. Rose walked around the room
while everyone worked.
He smiled.
He answered some questions.
But if someone asked if what they
were doing was *right*, he said,
"There's no one right way to wrap an egg."

Mr. Rose put some of the questions
he heard on the blackboard.

"Do eggs float?"

"Do they float in plain water?"

"In salt water?"

"Are some eggshells stronger than others?"

Jamie noticed there were still
two eggs left in the egg carton.
She said, "Mr. Rose, why don't you
try to wrap an egg, too?"

"Yeah," yelled Justin and Sarah
and Sally and Matt.

Everyone really wanted Mr. Rose to be
in the contest.

Except Adam.

He thought Mr. Rose would win.

"He's probably done this before," said Adam.

Mr. Rose promised that he hadn't.

"Everyone has an equal chance of winning,"
Mr. Rose said. "And as far as I'm concerned,
everyone who tries is a winner."

Adam felt better.

And Mr. Rose agreed to try to make a package
for an egg while helping the class.

23

Jennifer walked by Sarah's table.

It looked like everyone was cutting out circles.

Sarah was making hers out of cloth.

Sally was making hers out of paper.

"What are you making?" Jennifer asked.

"Parachutes," said Sarah. "Our eggs
    will be like sky divers."

Justin had found a really small box.
His egg fit perfectly inside.
He was trying to attach the box to the
parachute he had made.
It just didn't seem to work.
He asked Mr. Rose for help.
Mr. Rose said, "If you can't do it by yourself,
    I'll help. But try it on your own
    a little longer."

Richard came back to the room
carrying a pillow.
He must have borrowed it from
Mrs. Stone, the nurse.
Matt was so busy wrapping clay around his egg,
he didn't even notice that Richard was back.
Emily said, "Hey, Richard, how come you didn't
use what was on the science table?"
"I had a better idea," Richard answered.
Emily laughed. "I'd hate to sleep on that pillow
tonight, after your egg breaks in it!"

Sarah and Sally also were having a hard time. "Parachutes aren't easy," they said to each other.

"How are you going to win with a big box
like that?" Jamie asked Adam.
"The bigger the box, the more stuffing
it holds," answered Adam.
"But your egg will roll around," Emily said.
"Not if I pack it tight," Adam answered.
"You'll never do it right," said Jamie.
"You should put your egg inside a tennis ball,
like I did," said Emily.
"Oh, mind your own business," Adam said.
Mr. Rose reminded everybody to concentrate
on their own project.
Not much time left.
And not much stuff, either!

"Can you believe it?" Jennifer asked.

"No broken eggs yet!"

Jennifer was busy sealing her eggs tightly inside a plastic container filled with water. She was using tape.

"Don't use the whole roll!" Kelly shouted.

"I need tape, too!"

Kelly kept on talking. "Too bad Mr. Rose didn't give us paint. I think paint would keep this egg from cracking."

"Don't be silly!" said Jennifer. "It wouldn't make any difference!"

"How do you know until you experiment?" Kelly asked.

Mr. Rose agreed with Kelly. He said any idea was a good one until someone proved it wrong.

Mr. Rose said everybody had five minutes before clean-up time.
He told those who were done to bring their wrapped eggs to him.
He told everybody else to hurry.
At the count of twenty, the egg-drop contest would begin.
It was going to be interesting.
Very interesting.

CHAPTER THREE
THE CONTEST

Ten, nine,.eight, seven, six, five,
four, three, two, one...
Drop!
Mr. Rose dropped Sarah's egg out the window.
Everyone watched it fall.

"Here go the other two parachutes,"
  said Mr. Rose, as he launched Sally's
  egg and then Justin's egg.
They sailed smoothly to the ground.
No crash landings yet!
Sally and Justin smiled.
They were pretty sure their eggs hadn't broken.

Out the window went Adam's box
and Emily's tennis ball.
They quickly hit the ground.
Clunk!
Boing! Boing!
Adam and Emily wondered whether or not
their eggs were safe.
Mr. Rose stood at the window and said,
  "Listen for the sound of Richard's pillow.
    Here it goes!"

Matt's egg, wrapped in clay and foam rubber,
made a funny-shaped package.
Out the window it went.

Mr. Rose said "good-bye" when he dropped
Kelly's small paper bag.

Jennifer's plastic container was next.
It, too, went out the window.

"Just two more eggs to drop," Sarah said
    to Mr. Rose. "Yours and Jamie's."
"Drop mine last," said Jamie, who wanted
    to keep her egg safe in its box
    for as long as possible.
"All right," said Mr. Rose. "I'll drop
    mine first, then Jamie's."
Everyone watched the packages go.

"Can we go downstairs and start unwrapping?" Sarah asked.

"Yes," said Mr. Rose. "But walk, don't run. And be careful when you unwrap your eggs!"

"I don't want to open mine," Emily said.

"It's probably all yucky inside," said Justin.

Jamie said, "I think I'll wait until everyone else opens theirs."

"Why?" asked Richard.

"Because I don't want to be the first to find a cracked egg!" Jamie answered.

Unwrapping wasn't so easy.
The tape was hard to get unstuck.
The string was hard to get unknotted.
There were lots of layers to get through.
Matt was the first one to see his egg.
"It's okay!" he shouted.

"Mine's okay, too!" yelled Richard.
An egg in a pillow—not such a bad
idea after all.
Then, "UGH!"
Everyone heard it loud and clear.
Whose egg had cracked?

"It's Jennifer's!" Sarah said to Emily.
Jennifer liked to be first.
But she didn't like looking at
the first broken egg.
Too bad!
"Did you put salt in the water?"
    someone asked.
"No," answered Jennifer.
"Maybe you should have."
"It's too late now," said Jennifer,
    looking sadly at her cracked egg.
Too late.
But there was no reason why Jennifer
couldn't experiment again.
And the next time she could try
using salt water.

CHAPTER FOUR
WHO WON?

Sarah and Sally got to their eggs
at the same moment.
When Sarah put her hand inside the box
she had tied to the parachute, she said,
"It's wet!"

Sally said, "Mine's sticky!"

They both knew their eggs had cracked.

Mr. Rose asked them what they would do differently next time.

"I don't know," Sally said.

Mr. Rose said, "I don't like to hear you say *I don't know*. It means you're refusing to think."

"Well, maybe I could make a bigger parachute," said Sally.

"That sounds like a good idea," said Mr. Rose. "If one idea doesn't work, then it's always good to try something else."

"I will," said Sally. "I'm going to try some egg experiments on Saturday."

Justin did everything right this time.

His egg was perfect.

So was Kelly's.

And Adam's big box had worked after all.

The tennis ball kept Emily's egg safe.

"Hooray for me!" Emily shouted.

Then it was Mr. Rose's turn.

He had put rubber bands around his egg,

then stuffed it into an envelope.

Mr. Rose happily opened the envelope.

His smile soon turned into a frown.

His egg was leaking inside.

"See?" Jennifer said to Adam.

"Mr. Rose didn't win."

Sally quickly said, "If one idea doesn't work,

it's always good to try something else."

"I will," said Mr. Rose. "I'll do it

on Saturday, just like you!"

Jamie, as she had wished, had the last
unopened package.
She slowly lifted the lid of her small box.
She took out the shredded newspaper,
cotton, and pencil shavings.
"Hurry up!" someone yelled.
"So let's see it already!"
Jamie lifted her egg and held it
high in the air.
It was fine!

Mr. Rose asked everyone with unbroken eggs
to pose for a picture.
Justin, Matt, and Kelly kneeled
in the first row.
Emily, Adam, Richard, and Jamie
stood behind them.
"Smile, everybody," Mr. Rose said.
Click!

"Now the rest of us should pose together,"
   said Mr. Rose, "because we tried hard, too."
Sarah, Sally, and Jennifer stood next to Mr. Rose
as Matt took a picture.
Click!

Mr. Rose collected the eggs.

He didn't want them to break.

Then he said, "Everybody line up at the door.
We're going inside to talk about
the contest and have a snack."

Everyone cried out, "Aren't we going to have
a party? You promised!"

Mr. Rose smiled. "You're right! I promised
a party if you all worked hard today."

"And we did!" said Justin.

"I agree," said Mr. Rose. "So let's line up
for a party!"

"How should I tell Mrs. Brill to cook
the eggs?" Mr. Rose asked.

"I like mine hard-boiled—with ketchup!"
said Justin.

"Yuck!" said Sarah. "I prefer mustard."

"Mustard's okay with hot dogs," said Justin,
"but not with eggs."

"Deviled eggs have mustard," said Sally, who
seemed to know something about cooking.

"Who wants to try deviled eggs?" asked Mr. Rose.
No one raised a hand.

"If Mrs. Brill makes plain, hard-boiled eggs,
then you can add ketchup or salt
or mustard or peanut butter..."

"We get it," Justin interrupted Mr. Rose.
"What else can we have besides eggs?"

"Because this is a party, you can have soda
instead of juice. And you can have
two cookies instead of just one,"
answered Mr. Rose.

"What else can we have?" Sarah asked.

"A good time!" said Mr. Rose. "Maybe we can
play a game of Twenty Questions."

"Can we have another egg-drop contest?"
Richard asked.

"Not in school," said Mr. Rose. "But you can
try it at home if you get permission."

"I'm going to try something different," said Sally.
"I'll use my father's sneaker!"

Justin gave out the soda.
Emily passed around the straws;
Matt, the napkins.
Kelly counted the cookies—two for each person.
Then she handed them out.
"Can't we have more than two each?"
    Jennifer begged.
"Definitely not," said Mr. Rose.
"Where are the eggs?" Sarah asked.
"They should be ready soon," Mr. Rose said.
    "It takes about twenty minutes for them
        to hard-boil."

"I wish we were having egg-drop soup instead,"
said Sally.

"What's that?" Adam asked.

"I always order it in the Chinese restaurant,"
answered Sally. "I didn't think of it
before, but if Mr. Rose dropped eggs into
a pot of boiling water, instead of out
the window, we'd have egg-drop soup!"

"Sounds weird," said Adam. "I'm sure it would
taste a whole lot better if he dropped them
in a pot of my grandma's chicken soup."

"Too much talk about food!" said Emily.
"It makes me hungry. I wish we could eat
already!"

"While we're waiting for the eggs to be cooked,
    let's write down what happened today,"
    suggested Mr. Rose. "I'll start a chart."
"Why do we always have to make a chart?"
    Emily asked.
"Because it helps you understand what you know
    and don't know," answered Mr. Rose.
    Mr. Rose asked each person for a sentence
    and wrote down what was said.

. Mr. Rose gave us a challenge today.
. He challenged us to think of different ways to pack raw eggs.
. He dropped eleven eggs out the window.
. Four of them broke.
. Seven stayed whole.

Then Mr. Rose asked, "What did you learn?"

"I learned that some things protect eggs
better than others," answered Jennifer.
"Like plastic bubbles."

"But there was plastic bubble wrap in my
envelope," said Mr. Rose. "And my egg
still cracked."

"Well, it doesn't work all of the time,"
said Jennifer. "Only sometimes."

"Only sometimes," repeated Mr. Rose. "If we
wanted to say something more definite,
we'd have to make hundreds of trials."

"That would be expensive!" said Sally.

"And it would take a lot of time," added
Mr. Rose. "Today I only wanted to show
you that there are many ways to do the
same thing. I wanted you to be creative—
not sure of one right way to do it."

"I like being creative," said Sally. "It's fun!"

"And when you're creative, you usually end up
with a lot of questions," said Mr. Rose.
"So let's make a list."

There were a lot of questions.
Mr. Rose tried to write as fast as
everyone was talking.
What would happen if . . .
   we used brown eggs?
   we went to a higher floor?
   we painted the eggs first?
   we dropped each egg more than once?
How many ways are there to cook an egg?
Are eggs good or bad for you?
Why do only some eggs hatch?
How long does it take for an egg to hatch?
By the time there were no more questions,
Mr. Rose had filled the whole blackboard.
He said, "I'm not going to erase these questions
   for a few days so we can talk about them.
   In the meantime, you might want to tell
   your parents what we did today and find
   out what they know about eggs."

57

Mrs. Brill brought the eggs from the lunchroom.
Mrs. Brill cooled them under cold running water.
Then she took off the shells.
"We'll have to split these eggs because there
aren't enough to go around," said Mr. Rose.
He cut one of the eggs in half and said,
"Mrs. Brill, this yolk looks just right.
It's a perfect yellow."

"And there's no mushy middle!" said Jennifer.

"I'm glad," said Emily. "I hate hard-boiled
    eggs with mushy middles."

"Can we eat now?" asked Justin, who was starving.

"You can eat," said Mr. Rose. "Come and get
    salt or ketchup or mustard from the tray
    if you want it."

"No peanut butter?" Justin asked with a smile.

"No peanut butter," said Mr. Rose.
    "We can have it tomorrow with crackers."

Everyone ate pretty fast.

Then there was clean-up time.

Mr. Rose thought there was time for
one game of Twenty Questions.

Matt told the class he was thinking of an object.

"Does it have anything to do with what
we did today?" Sally asked.

Matt thought for a second. "Yes."

"Is it an egg?" everyone asked at once.

"No," said Matt. "That's one question."

"Is it a window?" asked Adam.

"No."

"Is it egg-drop soup?" Jamie asked.

"No."

"A parachute?" Sarah wondered.

"No."

Matt grinned. No one was going to guess
what he was thinking of.

Richard asked, "Is it a pillow?"

"No."

Soon there was only one question left.

"I know!" said Kelly. "It's a chicken!"

Matt frowned. "How did you guess?"

"Chickens and eggs go together,"
    Kelly answered.

"But which came first?" asked Richard.

"That's a good question," Mr. Rose said.
    "But we definitely don't have time for
    it today. Unless you all want to
    stay and have eggs for dinner."

No thanks!

"What are we going to do tomorrow?"
Matt asked.
"I have a good idea," said Mr. Rose,
"but I want to keep it to myself."
"Please tell," begged Jennifer.
"You can wait," answered Mr. Rose.
"You can wait until tomorrow."
Class dismissed.
See you Friday.

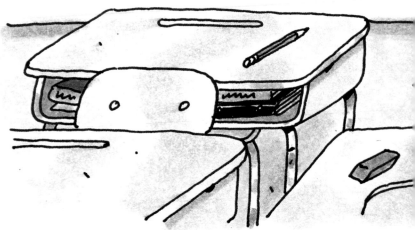

Homework

- Have an egg drop contest with members of your family.

- What kinds of eggs are sold at the market?

- What can you learn about eggs from reading the labels on the egg carton?

- Find some egg recipes and copy your favorite one. Cook an egg if you can.

Mr. Rose